May I Please Have a Cookie?

To Robin and Leo
—J.M.

Copyright © 2005 by Jennifer Morris.

All rights reserved. Published by Scholastic Inc.
SCHOLASTIC, CARTWHEEL BOOKS, and associated logos
are trademarks and/or registered trademarks of Scholastic Inc.
Lexile is a registered trademark of MetaMetrics, Inc.

Library of Congress Cataloging-in-Publication Data
Morris, J. E. (Jennifer E.)
  May I please have a cookie? / by J.E. Morris
    p. cm.
  "Cartwheel books."
  Summary: Alfie, a young alligator, learns the best way to ask for a
cookie from his mother.
  ISBN 0-439-73819-9
  [1. Etiquette — Fiction. 2. Alligators — Fiction. 3. Cookies — Fiction] I. Title.
  PZ7.M82824Ma 2005
  [E] — dc22   2004031113

ISBN-13: 978-0-439-73819-4
ISBN-10: 0-439-73819-9

58 57 56 55 54   18   19/0

Printed in the U.S.A. 40 • This edition first printing, September 2008

May I Please Have a Cookie?

by Jennifer E. Morris

SCHOLASTIC INC.

Mommy was baking cookies.

Alfie loved cookies.

He loved to smell cookies.

He loved to look at cookies.

But most of all, Alfie loved to eat cookies.

"Don't grab, Alfie," said Mommy.
"Can you think of a better way
to get a cookie?"

Alfie thought

and thought

and thought.

Then Alfie got
an idea.

He found a big coat
and a big hat.

"I want a cookie,"
said Alfie in a big,
deep voice.

Oops.

"No, Alfie," said Mommy.
"Think of a better way to get
a cookie."

Alfie had another idea.

He went outside.

Mommy put icing on the cookies.

Then she saw something.

"Get down, Alfie!"
cried Mommy.

"Think of a better way
to get a cookie."

Alfie thought of another idea.
He went to his room and got
some paper.

He cut and he colored.

Soon Alfie had his own cookies.

But he still wanted
a real cookie.

He began to cry.

Mommy hugged Alfie.
"Your cookies look yummy.
May I please have one?"

Then Alfie had the best idea of all.

"Mommy, may I please have a cookie?" he said.

"Yes, you may, Alfie," said Mommy

"Thank you," said Alfie.

"You're welcome," said Mommy.